AF392614

A Christmas Wish

SMALL-TOWN BRIDES

DIANA LESIRE BRANDMEYER

DKD BOOKS

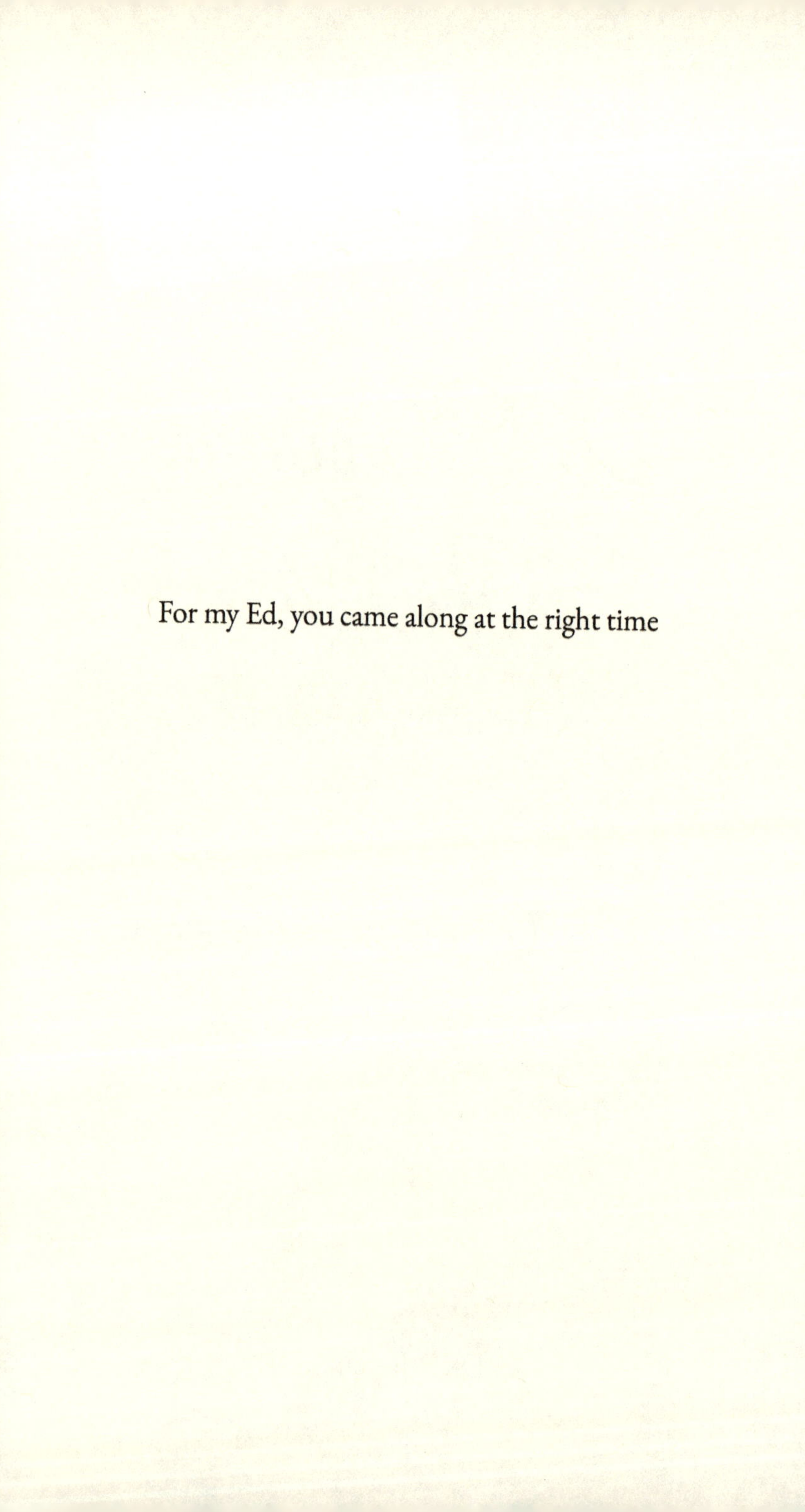

For my Ed, you came along at the right time

Copyright © 2021 by Diana Lesire Brandmeyer

All rights reserved.

No portion of this book may be reproduced in any form without written permission from the publisher or author, except as permitted by U.S. copyright law.

Contents

CHAPTER ONE

ROY GIBBONS STIRRED THE pot of oatmeal on the woodstove while doing his best to ignore the state of his kitchen.

"Papa, it shouldn't look like that." Eight-year-old Elisbet glared at him. "I can't wait until our Christmas mama gets here."

If Janie were here, everything would be in the cupboards where it belonged, not shoved into nooks and crannies. He never thought he'd be making breakfast for his daughters, much less trying to keep their frocks clean and pressed. He missed his wife more and more every day. Roy didn't know how she'd made his home run so smoothly. Not once had he needed to worry about how to get tomato stains off his shirt or when to cut his hair. She'd say in her musical voice, "It's time, sit down and let me trim that head, Roy."

When Elisbet asked him for a mother for Christmas, he'd said yes, thinking it couldn't be that hard to find one.

"Papa, do you think Becky will have sugar cookies at her party?" Frances, his youngest and his shadow, tugged his pant leg.

"Franny, she's going to have cake. That's what you have at a birthday party, right, Papa?" Elisbet never had trouble correcting her younger sister.

"But I like sugar cookies." Frances tugged again. "Can we make cookies when we come home? Mama makes the best kind."

"Mama *made* not makes. She's in heaven. Remember?" Elisbet patted her sister's shoulder. "When our Christmas mama comes, she'll make cookies with us."

"Stop telling her that, Elisbet. It's not that easy to get a mother. You can't wish for a mother and I can't order one from the catalog." He slid the pot from the burner, his little shadow still clinging to his leg as he moved. "Sit down, girls, and I'll fill your bowls." Roy was still stinging from Widow Percy's rejection. She'd have been a perfect fill-in for his deceased wife. Seemed logical—she didn't have a father for her boys, and his girls didn't have a mother. When he suggested they marry for the common good of their families, she'd done all but slap his face.

Trouble was, he hadn't lived here long enough to know people. Maybe he'd made a mistake moving here after Janie died. If he'd stayed in Collinsville, he'd have a mother for the girls by now. The whole reason he'd left was because too many young hopefuls were knocking on the door with some treat and mooning over him and the girls. At the time, he didn't want another wife. No one could fill Janie's shoes, and these women would be expecting to have children of their own. He couldn't face that, not after losing Janie and the baby. No, he didn't need a companion. Just someone to take care of his house and his family.

He scooped up the oatmeal and plopped a lump in each girl's bowl.

He sat at the head of the table, a daughter on either side of him, and pushed back the hurt that came from seeing Janie's chair at the other end. The house was different, but the spot across the table was as empty as if he hadn't left Collinsville. "Grace, then food." He watched until little hands were folded and heads bowed, then said the prayer followed by an "Amen."

Frances stuck her fingers on the inside of her bowl to pull it closer. "Hot!" The bowl went spinning from the table to her lap and then crashed to the floor. She wailed.

"Are you all right? Are your fingers burned?" Roy sprung from his chair and pulled his daughter from hers. He grabbed her hands and flipped them palm up. They weren't red. Relieved to avoid a crisis, he planted a kiss on her fingertips the way he'd seen Janie do so many times.

"My dress," Frances whimpered. "It's dirty. I don't have another one for the party."

"Shh, Frances, stop crying. Your fingers look fine, and no one will notice your dress." Kneeling, he reached under the table for the offending bowl and spoon that had spoiled Frances's morning.

"If we had a mama, this wouldn't have happened, Papa." Elisbet already held a wet rag in her hand. She dabbed at her sister's dress. "It's only a little bit of oatmeal. Look, Franny. See? I got it off."

It bothered him that Elisbet tried to be like Janie, and he had no idea how to prevent it.

"But it's my favorite and it's. . ." Frances hiccupped. "Wet!"

Roy wondered how he would ever raise these girls without help.

Alma Pickens tugged her cape closer to guard against the sharp fangs of the November wind and leaned across the buggy seat. Her father had returned to the very subject she'd asked him not to speak about at breakfast. "Papa, you're a dreamer. Maybe I'm not the only one God will send a spouse for. I do believe I'll pray as hard as you do for me, that you'll marry again. A doctor should have a wife."

And she would take it to God in her prayers. She'd grown weary of her father's constant efforts to see her married. It wasn't that she was against the idea, but she'd made a promise to her mother to take care of him. And it would be a rare man who would marry her and take in her father as well.

Besides, she had her painting and taking care of her father's home. That gave her plenty to do. Why, just this morning she'd risen earlier than normal and put in a full day's work so she could come to town with him despite the cold to make a deposit at the bank and to visit her friend Jewel.

"Little Bit, it's not right for you to devote your life to me."

"Papa, I told you not to worry about me. I have you, and I don't need anyone else. Besides, there isn't anyone left in Trenton that I'd care to marry."

"Alma, my girl, you'll make a good wife and mother. I can't sit back and watch you miss out. God will bring someone." He stopped the horse in front of Bossman's Bank and stepped out of the wagon. He tied the horse to the hitching post and helped Alma dismount. "I'm too old to get married again. It's you I worry about. I'll pick you up at Jewel's when I'm through at the Detterman's. And don't start making lists of promising wives for me. Go on, get in the bank and put your pennies away."

"I'm going." Who would be a good match for him? And who could she find that wouldn't mind her presence in the house as well?

Maybe she should hold off ordering from the Montgomery Ward catalog. She had her heart set on the Oil Painting Outfit Complete. It was outrageously expensive, but it came with twenty-five colors of paint. If she weren't able to sell her paintings right away, and her father married a woman who valued their privacy, she would need that money to rent a room somewhere. And without the paints and lessons that came with the painting outfit, how would she have anything to sell? Well, she wouldn't worry about that today, seeing as how there weren't any women who interested Papa. The irony that this town held no one for either of them struck her. Maybe Papa would consider moving to St. Louis, where her paintings would be discovered, and she'd be famous and wealthy. He could be a doctor there, and the number of people in that city would increase his chance of finding another wife.

She needed to talk this new idea of St. Louis over with Jewel. Together they'd find a solution.

~ello~

Inside the bank, Alma waited her turn. Two little blond girls in front of her clung to their father. She knew who they were—the Gibbons family minus the mother who had died last spring giving birth. Mrs. Remik at the store said everyone was speculating on when Mr. Gibbons would take another wife to help with Elisbet and Frances.

The oldest, Elisbet, played peekaboo with her sister. Their giggles captured one hiding in Alma. She clenched her lips to contain it, but it escaped.

Mr. Gibbons turned and smiled. Alma had an unusual urge to slide her finger into the indentation on his cheek. Dimples. Then she noticed what looked like oatmeal in his hair. She shuddered. The man needed help.

"I apologize if my girls disturbed you, miss."

"They didn't. Their giggles captivated me along with those dark blue eyes." If she were painting them, she'd use cobalt blue to capture their intensity.

"We're going to a birthday party," Elisbet said.

Alma leaned down. "I love birthday parties, lots of games and cake to eat."

"I have oatmeal on my dress." Frances looked so sorrowful that Alma wanted to take her down to the store and buy her a new frock.

"Franny, it's okay. Remember I got it off and your dress dried on the way here. Papa, we have to get Becky a gift, don't forget. I want to get her red hair ribbons."

Had that man brought his daughter out in this cold weather with a wet dress? Was he touched in the head? No doubt her own father would end up at their place tending to the little girl for pneumonia.

"I don't. I think we should get her a knife." Frances held up her hands and pretended to open one. "It would be grand to have one. Papa, can I have one for my birthday?"

"We'll see. We best get moving if there's shopping and lunch to do yet." He turned to Alma. "Nice to meet you."

"Papa, can she be the mama you're getting us for Christmas? She doesn't have a wedding ring. I looked like you showed me." Elisbet smiled a got-you-now smile at her father.

Mr. Gibbons's green eyes flashed to Alma's, and his face flushed. "Let's go, girls." He ushered them out without another word to Alma.

Alma watched them leave, noticing the hem on Elisbet's coat was torn. She understood the child's desire for a mother, but sincerely hoped her father didn't run into Mr. Gibbons before Christmas.

CHAPTER TWO

R OY COVERED F RANCES ' S SHIVERING body with the
blanket from his bedroom and tucked it around her.
Her teeth chattered, and he brushed his hand against her
forehead. Hot. Nothing good ever came from fevers. He
couldn't let his daughters see his worry, especially Elisbet.
"You'll be right as rain soon. I sent Pete to fetch the doctor.
He'll be here before long."

"Not the doctor!" Frances sobbed. "I want Mama."

Her words cut through him, opening a scar he'd thought
healed. "We all do. The doctor will help you feel better,
sweetheart." He'd taken to calling his daughters by the
terms of endearment he'd heard Janie use. It seemed to
settle them down when they were in a state he didn't
understand. He should never have left Collinsville. Right
now, his mother could be helping him with this sick child.

Frances coughed again and again. Her body shook, and
her chest had a rattle Roy didn't like. "Elisbet, sit and read

to your sister until the doctor and Pete get here or I get done milking the cows."

Elisbet, eyes wide and face pale, didn't object but grabbed the picture book Frances loved. "Can I get under the covers with Franny?"

"I want Elisbet!" Frances threw off the covers.

Frances didn't know what she wanted, but he would give her what he could. "Didn't I just tuck you in, little girl?"

"Please, Papa?" Frances coughed again.

Roy slid back the covers. "Climb in." He waited for Elisbet to snuggle in next to her sister. *Please God, don't let her get sick, too.* "I'll be back as soon as I can."

Roy knew Elisbet was terrified. He wished he didn't understand her fear, but he did—all too well. The last time they'd seen a doctor, Janie died. He left his heart with his daughters as he headed outside. You couldn't let a cow go unmilked, even if you had somewhere better to be.

He shivered. He should have grabbed his coat. No matter, the barn would hold back the chill. He'd have to keep Elisbet home from school tomorrow to help him with Frances. He couldn't take care of a sick child, do barn chores, and work at the mill. This illness pushed him to fulfill his daughters' Christmas wish. He'd write to his mother, asking her who back home was still looking to get married. He wanted a widow, someone who'd already known love and didn't expect it to happen again. Someone who'd understand she couldn't replace his wife any more than he could replace her husband.

Alma convinced her father to take her for an afternoon drive before the winter snows came and forced them to stay close to town. Outside of town, the roads suffered from last week's gully washer, making the smooth rides of summer a memory to be cherished. The buggy springs bounced, squeaking as the wheels dipped in and out of holes in the dirt road. Alma held on to the edge of her seat. "Thanksgiving makes me sad. It makes me think of Mama."

"I think about her every day. Holidays are the hardest for me. But you've your mother's happy attitude about life, and that helps me." Her father winked at her. "Yes, you do many things that remind me of her."

"Tell me how, Papa." Alma drew the buggy blanket up higher on her lap. The warmth of fall had been shoved aside as winter gained a foothold. The trees held tight to a few weather-beaten leaves. Another strong wind and they'd be bare.

"The way you want to make small things into a celebration. Like Thursday, you invited friends to eat with us, but it wasn't enough to have all those platters of food. You decorated the table with red and gold leaves. That's not something I would do."

"Too many germs, Dr. Pickens? Those tiny little things no one can see?" Alma tried to raise an eyebrow the way her father did when making a point. It wouldn't go.

Dr. Pickens raised his brow. "Still can't do it? Neither could your mother. And yes, there is a new study out about germs being in unexpected places. It's possible leaves would carry bacteria spores, but your happiness matters more to me, so I kept quiet."

"Thank you. The decorations made the entire dinner party more festive. If the leaves make people sick, wouldn't everyone be ill when they fall from the trees?"

"It does seem I have more patients in the winter, doesn't it?"

"That's because it's cold and we don't get enough fresh air. You taught me that. So I'm like you, too, Papa."

"I'd like you to be more like your mother and me—married."

This conversation was going down a corduroy road she didn't wish to travel. Distraction always worked with her father. "Who was the letter from that you were reading last night?"

"Someone you don't know. How about Mr. Bruin? He'd make a good husband."

"I can't marry him. I won't. I know you're concerned for me, but I'd never be happy married to a miner. I'm surprised you would even consider him. He must bring home lots of germs every night. Why, I could catch something and die before spring if I were to marry him." She tried one more time to arch her eyebrow. It wouldn't go, so she pushed it up with her finger.

In the distance, Alma saw a horse and a rider coming up on them fast. "Look, someone else is out for a ride today."

"Doesn't appear he's riding for fun. Must be an emergency. He's got that horse running at a gallop." Dr. Pickens pulled back on the reins. "Wise to slow down and let him pass. No need to give our boy Charlie here a reason to bolt."

The horseback rider whipped off his hat and waved. "Dr. Pickens! We need you at the Gibbonses'." He stopped his horse next to the buggy.

"Pete, you came up so fast I didn't recognize you. What's the problem?"

"Roy Gibbons's little one is sick. She can't stop coughing, and he said she's burning hot as a barn afire. He sent me to get you. Can you come straight away?"

Her father wore his serious face; she knew he wouldn't hesitate.

"We'll follow you." Doctor Pickens urged Charlie into a trot.

"What does Mr. Gibbons do for a living, Papa?"

"I heard he bought Becker's farm." His forehead furrowed like a freshly plowed field.

"He's not married. Jewel says he never comes to town without the girls. Why do you suppose that is?"

"I take you places."

"Yes, but not all the time. Do you think he's taking care of the girls by himself? That would explain the oatmeal in his hair and the torn hem."

"Oatmeal? What are you talking about?"

"I saw them at the bank. The girls were going to a birthday party and were excited, but they weren't dressed for the occasion. I wanted to take them home, curl their hair, and buy them pretty dresses. I hope the other children weren't mean to them."

"Were they mean to you?" Her father's mouth turned down.

She hadn't meant to hurt him. "No. Well, sometimes. It didn't happen after you asked for help from Mrs. Wilson."

"She was a saint to step in. I'm not sure you would have learned how to be a lady if not for her."

"You tried, Papa." Alma pushed back memories of the times she missed her mother. She'd kept many of them from her father.

The two-story farmhouse appeared when they came around the bend in the road. A house built for a large family, not a father and two little girls. "Will you let me help?"

"Don't believe you've become a doctor since lunch, have you?"

"No."

"You can carry my bag."

"I'm no longer a child."

"Believe me, I'm aware."

The door opened, and Mr. Gibbons stepped onto the porch. "In here, Doctor. Franny is sick. I don't know what to do."

Alma followed her father into the house. She'd learned early to step back when her father was needed. Too many times she'd landed on the floor as he rushed by her.

Mr. Gibbons hadn't waited for either of them, but it wasn't difficult to locate him or the patient. The coughing led them to the sick child.

Dr. Pickens felt Frances's forehead. "Definitely a fever. You need to take those blankets off of her right now. You're making the fever climb higher. I need a basin of cold water and a cloth, please."

When Mr. Gibbons removed the covers, Frances cried out. "I'm cold!"

Alma rushed to the child's side and stroked her arm. "Do you like to build snowmen? I bet you're as cold as one, aren't you?"

Frances quieted. "Yes."

"Mr. Gibbons, the water please?" Papa dug in his black bag. It was a good thing he'd acquired the habit of tossing it into the buggy whenever he left home.

Alma spoke to Mr. Gibbons. "I'll watch over her while you're gone. It won't take but a minute to get what Papa needs."

He nodded and hastened from the room. Alma felt compassion for the man. Not having a wife to help him through this trying time had to be difficult. Had it been like this for her father?

"I'm cold."

"Keeping the covers on will make you sicker longer. Then you'll be sad if it snows and you can't go outside to build a snowman." Alma sat on the bed next to Frances and picked up a book. "Were you reading this?"

"Sissy read it to me."

"Where is Sissy?"

Frances pointed to the corner where Elisbet stood, her eyes focused on Alma's father. She seemed frozen in fear.

Alma smoothed Frances's hair. "My papa will take good care of you. Right now, I'm going to talk to Sissy." She went to Elisbet and knelt in front of her.

She grasped the child's hand. "You don't need to be afraid. My papa is a good doctor. He can make your sister well. Do you want to watch?"

Elisbet yanked her hand away, eyes wide. "No! She's going to die like Mama."

"No, she's not going to die." Roy strode into the room in time to hear Elisbet. "Right, Doc? Tell them everything is going to be fine." *Tell me, too.* He couldn't bear losing Frances. *God, please don't take her, too.* He'd been praying for her to get better. But then, he'd prayed for Janie, and it didn't make a difference.

Dr. Pickens removed the stethoscope from around his neck and returned it to his bag. "She'll be fine. She's got the croup. Feed her soup and give her tea with honey to soothe her throat and cough. I have a tincture you'll need to give her three times a day."

"Will Elisbet catch this, too?" If both girls were sick, he wouldn't be able to work at the mill. As it was, the idea of leaving Elisbet alone with Franny caused him some concern.

"She might. If she does, follow the same procedure. Keep a cool cloth on Frances's forehead for the night. Dip it in cold water when it warms. That will help bring down her fever. Keep her in bed for a few days."

"I don't have to go to school?" Frances propped herself up on her elbows.

"Then I'm not going either." Elisbet strutted from the corner. "I'll take care of Franny."

"We'll discuss it when the doctor has gone."

"Mr. Gibbons, do you have someone to watch the girls?" Dr. Pickens asked. "They are too small to stay home alone."

"I don't have a choice. You don't understand. It's the three of us that look out after each other."

"I'll watch them."

He turned and noticed the doctor's daughter was the woman from the bank. She held Elisbet's small hand in hers. It took him back in time. Janie with her daughters. Would it hurt them to have another woman look after them? Would they become attached, or worse, badger her about marrying him?

"Please, Papa?"

"Pretty please, Papa?"

Roy rubbed his forehead. He needed help. He'd deal with the consequences later.

Chapter Three

Alma's father waited in the buggy at the Gibbons farm. The sun cracked open the morning sky. Alma had brought fresh eggs, since she wasn't sure what their pantry held.

Mr. Gibbons met her with a finger over his lips. "They're still sleeping." He yawned. "Sorry, I was up most of the night."

"Is Frances better? Papa wants to know before he drives back to town."

"I think so. She doesn't feel as hot this morning, and she's not restless."

She turned and waved to her father. He tipped his hat in her direction and jiggled the reins. Charlie shook his head, pawed the ground, and the buggy wheels turned.

She didn't smell coffee brewing. "You haven't eaten?"

"No, you woke me up. It's a good thing, too. I need to do the barn chores first. I would have been late to work if you hadn't come when you did."

Alma held out the basket she'd brought along. "I brought eggs. If you don't mind, I can make breakfast." She didn't think twice about offering, but the grin on Mr. Gibbons's face said she'd given him a large gift.

"You wouldn't mind?" He was already sticking his arms into his coat sleeves.

"Not at all." Especially if he kept flashing those dimples at her.

"None of us are too picky about food. If you can make the oatmeal, I'd appreciate it." He took off out the door.

The minute she walked into the kitchen, Alma knew Mr. Gibbons didn't have a woman helping him. The stove was filthy, and there were dishes caked with dried oatmeal stacked on the table. She shrugged off her cloak and searched for an apron. Mr. Gibbons had left a shirt draped over a chair. With a sigh, she tied the sleeves around her waist. Not the best use of a shirt, but maybe it would save her favorite day dress.

She stoked the stove and put on the coffee. Next, she gathered the dirty dishes and put them in the sink to soak. She hadn't had breakfast either, and she hated oatmeal. There had to be something else for her to make that would be easy for Frances to eat. A quick search of the food supply and she had the makings for griddle cakes. The syrup would go down Frances's throat easier than lumpy oatmeal.

She found a clean bowl and mixed the ingredients.

"What are you doing?" Elisbet, hair tousled and in her nightclothes, peeked around the corner.

"Griddle cakes. Do you and your sister like them?"

"Better than oatmeal." Elisbet skipped across the floor. "Can I help?"

"Can you get out the griddle for me?"

Elisbet disappeared into the pantry and brought out the heavy cast-iron piece. "I can grease it. Mama showed me how."

"That would be helpful, thank you. Before you do that, could you get dressed and check to see if your sister is awake?"

"She's sleeping, but I bet she wakes up when she smells these cooking. Don't grease it, promise?"

"I promise. Off you go, and put on some warm clothes. It's cold today."

While the batter was resting, Alma started cleaning. She was wiping down the table when Mr. Gibbons came in the back door.

"Thanks for starting breakfast. I can finish up."

"I'm making griddle cakes, not oatmeal."

His dimples came out to torment her again. She needed a diversion. "Why don't you check on Frances? See if you can get her to come to breakfast?"

"You have flour on your face." Mr. Gibbons reached over and brushed her cheek, then withdrew his fingers fast, as if he'd been burnt. He whirled around and headed for the bedroom, muttering something about checking on Frances.

Alma touched her cheek where his fingers had been. If she were made of butter, she'd be a puddle on the floor.

Next to the window in her bedroom sat Alma's art studio. She'd tried to capture the playfulness of the barn kittens from last spring. The laundry basket looked right, but the kittens in it were giving her a great amount of difficulty. Jewel had been instrumental in helping her find an outlet for her creativity after her attempt at weaving palm leaves together to make hats failed.

Would it be easier to paint children? Frances and Elisbet would make good subjects, with their big blue eyes and blond curls. Curls that were a mess. After she'd cleaned the kitchen to a tolerable standard, she'd spent the rest of the day with the girls. She'd combed and braided their hair, even found ribbons to tie at the ends.

Their imaginations sparked hers, and they made up stories of castles and trolls. She could feel how they wanted her attention, and she was happy to give it. She prayed Elisbet's Christmas wish would come true, and they would get a mother.

Splat. Black paint hit the canvas in the wrong spot and trailed like a tear. She ought not to be thinking of those little ones. God would see to them. After all, He'd helped her father take care of her.

As the sun set, the light faded from golden to silver, making it difficult to see. Alma set her paintbrush and palette on the table next to her easel. Time to stop for today, which, by the look of the work she had accomplished this afternoon, was a good thing. Kittens shouldn't have cone-shaped heads, but she couldn't quite get them more rounded. Frustrated, she removed her painting apron and draped it over the chair. She had to get that painting kit and discover how to do it correctly.

Heavyhearted, she headed to the kitchen. On Wednesdays, she always made stew. Papa made calls that day and was often late to dinner, which gave her time to work on her art.

She couldn't let the problem of the kittens' misshapen heads alone. How did other painters get those round shapes? How did they paint children's heads? Did they trace something until they learned to do it freehand? Maybe she could use one of her mother's china cups. But would a real artist resort to something so amateur? She would ponder that. Maybe for this painting it would be okay. The next time she saw Jewel, she'd inquire about the rules. She was determined to be a real artist, not just occupy her time, even though that's what Papa said she was doing.

Her shoulders drooped. If this painting didn't sell, he would surely start talking about husbands again. He'd given her three choices and asked her to pick one. She shuddered. She'd known all of them since grade school and had never been fond of any of them.

She gave the stew a quick stir. The kitchen felt closed in and dark this evening. There were so many things she wanted to do in here. Despite being dirty, the Gibbons' kitchen was cheerful and full of light. Jewel had painted candlesticks with sunflowers in her kitchen and planned to paint her hutch with flowers. It was time to broach the topic with Papa again about brightening up this room.

Could she convince him to let her paint the corner cabinet?

He hated change. If you asked her, he lived too much in the past. Mama wasn't going to come back to life and complain about the look of the kitchen. Not when she was living in heaven, where everyone knew Christ had built her a mansion. Mama must love it there, all those bright colors and the sparkles on the streets. It was a shame they couldn't experience a bit of that here at home.

"It's time for a change. I'll tell him right after supper. I live here, too, and since neither of us is getting married and I do the cooking, the kitchen is as good as mine." Her hand flew to her mouth. Had she said that out loud? It was a good thing Papa wasn't lurking around the corner. He'd think she was daft. No, best find a way to ease into this change. He was a stubborn man, set in his ways, and his rules applied in this house. Maybe she should go to St. Louis on her own and take painting classes. That's what Jewel suggested, but Alma couldn't leave. Not when she'd promised to watch over him. Which brought her back to her plan of finding Papa a wife.

Alma stirred the stew again. Papa was late, and she didn't know if she should continue to keep the food warm. Sometimes when he stayed out this long, the family that needed him fed him.

The back door creaked open, and she spun around. The air rushed in, making the kerosene flames dance in their glass, casting graceful shadows across the room. "Papa, you're so late. What happened? Did you deliver a baby?"

"Not tonight. Is supper still warm?"

"Yes, but I do believe I'll warm it a bit more for you."

"Not too long, I'm hungry. Been looking forward to a hearty meal tonight." Papa took off his coat, slung it over his bent arm, and grabbed his hat. "I'll put these away later." He dropped them on a kitchen chair and sat at the table. "How was your afternoon?"

Papa asking about her day before eating sent a shiver up Alma's back. He was up to something. Food always came before conversation. She turned to face him. "You know that it's painting day. Are you getting too old to remember? It's a good thing you have me around to help you through your days."

He had the grace to flush and bend his head. Yes, there was something he was about to say, and Alma knew she wouldn't like it.

"Don't sass me, Alma. I was being polite."

"I'm sorry, Papa. I was teasing. Your last call must have been difficult. You haven't complained about my joshing with you in a long time. Did you lose a patient? Would you like me to make you some cocoa?"

"Forgive me for snapping at you. It's been a long day." He scrubbed his hands across his face. "There's something I need to tell you, and I know you won't like it, but what's done is done. We'll discuss it later, after I've eaten."

Alma slid a plate of stew across the table in front of her father and took a seat. "What do you mean, it's done? And what does it have to do with me?"

Chapter Four

WHAT'S DONE IS DONE? Inside Alma, tension built like steam collecting in a covered pot of boiling water. If Papa didn't finish his stew soon, she was going to snatch it off the table. How dare he drop a loaded statement that begged for questions and then say he'd discuss it with her as soon as he'd finished his supper? For once she was glad she hadn't remembered to make the biscuits.

Chew and swallow. Her father ate slower than a snake swallowing a mouse. "Papa, can't you tell me anything?"

Dr. Pickens held up a finger and shook his head no.

Alma jumped from her chair. "I don't understand why you would keep something from me. It must be unpleasant, or you would have told me straight away. This isn't like you." She tugged her ear.

"Don't pull on your ear."

Her hand dropped to her side. It had taken her years to break that tugging habit, and with one sentence Papa brought back her insecurities.

"You'll know soon enough. I want to eat and think about how I want to say what I have to say."

"Eat faster, please, because I'm imagining all kinds of things." Alma paced the kitchen, which gave her no satisfaction, since it only took four steps to cross the room. She slid back into her chair, propped her elbows on the table, and then rested her chin on her palms. Fine. She'd wait him out by staring at him.

He didn't look her in the eye or tell her to remove her elbows from the table. Alma refused to change her position. Even if it wasn't working, it made her feel like she was doing something.

When the last bit of stew disappeared, Alma grabbed the bowl. "Let me put this in the sink."

Her father squinted at her, then frowned. "Why do you have feathers in your hair?"

"I was creating a new hair ornament."

"Did you glue them in?"

"No, I glued them to a leather strip, but the glue wasn't quite dry and some of the feathers stuck. I'll get them out. Like most of the things I attempt to create, this was a failure, but I'm not giving up my creative works. Are you ready to tell me what you mean by 'what's done is done'?"

Dr. Pickens wiped his chin with a napkin and scooted his chair away from the table. "I've made a decision. I've signed up for a surgical course in St. Louis."

"St. Louis!" Alma clapped her hands. "That's wonderful! It will be a perfect place for us to live. Why, Jewel and I were discussing this on Saturday. When do we have to leave?"

"I'm leaving at the end of the year. You aren't."

"I don't understand."

"You can't go with me. I'm renting a room by the school."

"How long will you be gone? You don't need to worry. I can watch over the house."

"No, you can't. I've rented it out. I'll be gone a year, and you, my dear, will be getting married before I leave."

Anger chased fear down her back like a cat running over piano keys. "Married? Who to? Papa! This is so wrong. I don't want to get married, you know that."

"So you've said. It's my job as a father to make sure you are taken care of, and that's what I've done."

"Who did you pick? The man who works at Bassler Brewery and stumbles home at night? The coal miner who coughs so much he's probably going to die soon? Or the man who beats his dog?"

"Daughter, I listened to you."

His forehead wrinkled the way it did when he was concerned for her. Could it be he would change his mind? Alma stacked reasons why she needed to go with him to St. Louis, ready to use them all. "Good, then let's put this leaving me behind business away. There will—"

"Stop. I'm not finished. Yes, your reasons were sound for not picking one of those men. I've found a better one. Roy Gibbons. He's a good family man and goes to church. With Pastor Elrich's help, I obtained his mother's address. She wrote back. He's a good man and moved here to remove himself from memories of his deceased wife. The two of you are well suited. We've shaken hands. There will be a marriage."

* * *

Roy had hoped the dishes he'd tossed in to soak after dinner would clean up quick. He was wrong. Dried food seemed to have planted roots in the stoneware. He noticed the kitchen had lost the appetizing appeal it had held after Alma had cleaned it.

He used a knife to scratch the surface of the plate. Marrying Alma would solve quite a few problems. She wasn't a widow, but she seemed to like Elisbet and Frances. They'd taken to her, too. He could keep his Christmas promise to them. That made him smile. He'd wanted to tell them tonight, but decided to wait until after Dr. Pickens talked to Alma.

As far as he was concerned, a quick trip to see the minister after work one day next week would work out well. They'd be married, and Alma could start helping out right away. He'd already been through the courting of a woman and a wedding. He paused his chipping at the dried food. It had been nice the first time, but now it would be a waste of time. He and Alma would get to know each other after they were married.

Unless she expected to be courted. Her father had avoided that question when Roy brought it up. He'd said, "Alma will be happy to get married. She knows the little ones need a mother's care as soon as possible."

Seems her mother had died when she was a young'un. He went back to prying off the dried eggs. Roy figured God had sent him to Trenton because He knew Alma was here. That had to be it. A woman as pretty as she should be married by now, with children of her own.

Why wasn't she? Was there something wrong with her? Maybe she was too picky about whom she wanted to marry? Add that to her father being willing to let her get married without a courting period.

It had been his experience with Janie that women didn't always say what they wanted. Perhaps this Alma was different? She must be, or her father wouldn't be so confident in arranging this marriage without talking to her first.

~ele~

"All you have is the word of his mother? What mother would say anything bad about her son?" Alma sucked in her anger.

"You might have a point about that, but like I said, I've seen how he treats his daughters. I figure how he takes care of them is a good indication of what he'll be like as a husband."

"So I can go around with dried oatmeal in my hair and the hem of my dress torn and dragging in the streets?"

"Alma, calm down. You'll fix those things as their mother. What I see is the way he gets them candy at the store, the way the littlest one hangs onto his pants leg and he doesn't mind. The oldest holds his hand while they walk into church."

"So as long as I have candy, hang on his pants leg, and hold his hand, I'll be treated special as his wife?"

"Alma Gail Pickens. Enough. The matter is settled. He'll be over here tomorrow to discuss the details with you. I've given my word that you'll marry him, and there won't be a fuss about not having a season of courting."

"And I have no say in this? I'm to marry him without knowing him? Without being in love?"

"There isn't time for courting. I'm leaving the day after Christmas, and I want this settled before then." Dr. Pickens reached across the table for his daughter's hand. "I promise, you'll grow to love each other."

Tears stung her eyes. "But I promised Mama that I'd take care of you."

"I know, and you have done that longer than you should. Mr. Gibbons is a good man and needs help. You saw that; you even told me about the sad state of his home and how his daughters are taken with you."

"That doesn't mean he's the marrying kind!" She yanked her hand away from him and pushed back her chair. Married by Christmas might be what her father and Mr. Gibbons wanted, but not her.

"You know that's false, Alma. Think about what you're saying. He's been married before, and from what I can tell, still loves his wife. That means a lot to me. I'm glad. I feel good about handing you over to him."

"Glad? You're glad about giving me to a man who still loves another?"

"Yes, to me it means he's wanting to have the same kind of comfort and companionship he had before."

"Does that mean you didn't love Mama enough to want to marry again?"

"No, it means I never found someone I could love as much. Roy Gibbons has."

"I don't believe that. I won't do it." She snatched up the stew pan and scraped the metal spoon against the sides, not caring how much noise it made. She pushed the scraps into the garbage pail. She wasn't saving any leftovers. As far as she was concerned, Papa could make his own dinner from now on. See how glad he'd be about that.

Chapter Five

Roy thought it best to meet with Miss Pickens without his daughters. He'd left them with Pete, his farmhand. To their delight, Pete promised to take them out to play with the barn cats. They were so excited they forgot to ask where he was going and why they couldn't come with him. Even Frances had let go of his leg and attached herself to Pete.

Dr. Pickens's two-story brick home was much nicer than his. Guess it made sense to be located close to town where most of the people lived, quicker to get to emergencies. He raised his hand to knock on the door and then lowered it. Maybe this wasn't a good idea. It seemed reasonably sound yesterday, but now that he'd slept on it, the idea of marrying so quick felt wrong. His shoulders tightened. He and Miss Pickens would benefit from this arrangement. But would she like living on a farm so far from town? In a house that seemed too small when Frances and Elisbet got to squealing and shrieking? He'd given the doc his word, though, so he best follow through. He and Miss Pickens wouldn't be the first couple necessity had brought to the altar.

He tapped on the door, deciding a polite knock would be best. He stepped back and waited.

Miss Pickens opened the door. "Mr. Gibbons."

"Miss Pickens, your father suggested we meet this evening."

"Yes, he did."

Wasn't she going to ask him inside? "May I come in?"

She swung the door wide. "Please do. Papa is in the kitchen."

He'd remembered her blond hair, and that's about all. When she'd rescued him during Frances's illness, he hadn't noticed her dark blue eyes or how the top of her head didn't come up to his shoulder. "I came to see you, not him."

"Perhaps you did, but since the two of you have arranged my life for me, you might as well work out the details and fill me in later." She turned, back straight, and walked away from him like royalty. "Shut the door behind you."

So this wouldn't be as easy as the doc suggested. Miss Pickens would be a challenge. He closed the door, and for the first time in quite a while found himself excited about the prospect of winning a woman's attention.

— ℓℓ —

Alma, still spitting mad, led Mr. Gibbons into the kitchen where her father waited. "Mr. Gibbons is here. I think you two should chat and then let me know when I'm to leave the house."

"Alma, that's not how this is going to work. I know you're angry, but sit and get to know him before you stomp upstairs." Dr. Pickens pulled out a chair for her. "Evening, Roy."

"Doc." Roy stooped his shoulders to get through the doorway.

Alma hadn't noticed before how tall he stood or the width of his chest. The man and his dimples took her breath away. Maybe it wouldn't be so bad being married to him. At least she'd have something worth looking at every day. She found her way to the chair her father stood behind and sat. "Thank you. How are the girls?"

Roy sat across the table from her. "They're fine. Pete's letting them play with the barn cats while I'm here."

"What do they think of you getting married?" She heard the terse tone in her voice and didn't like it. She'd been taught better than this. "Love your neighbor as yourself" came to mind.

Dr. Pickens slid a cup of coffee onto the table in front of Mr. Gibbons and gave Alma a look she knew too well as he handed her one. She had taken this as far as she could.

"I know they are anticipating a mother for Christmas, so I wondered about their excitement at the news." There, that was better.

"I haven't told them. Thought I ought to talk to the woman I was marrying first and make sure there would be a wedding." He gave her a slow grin, then took a sip of his drink.

He'd considered her feelings? Her heart fluttered. She hadn't expected that. "I don't understand. I thought. . ."

"Well, I agreed to marry you, but not until after I decided you would be interested. I can't be bringing home just anyone to be a mother to my daughters. There are enough fairy tales out there to scare them without getting them their own wicked stepmother."

"But. . ."

"Sorry, Miss Pickens, I didn't mean to imply that you would be like that. I think it best for both parties to be agreeable to marriage." He set his cup down. "What about you?"

Alma's tongue-twisted words couldn't make it past her lips. He had to be the most beautiful man she'd ever been this close to. She wrenched herself out of an imaginary embrace and felt the loss. "I—I think. . .yes."

Mr. Gibbons slapped his hands together, making her jump. "Then we have a deal. You're right, Doc, she did say yes."

Alma gasped.

"I talked to the reverend, and we can get married Sunday, Miss Pickens."

"No!" Alma's stomach contents slid and jerked, bumping into her throat. "Not Sunday. I have a few things to say about this wedding, and the first thing is—it won't be this weekend."

Roy couldn't be more confused. The woman had said she'd marry him. Why would she want to delay? Her father had said courting her wasn't necessary.

"Mr. Gibbons, I will marry you on Christmas Eve."

"Why wait? Four weeks isn't going to change anything, and I need a wife now."

"I refuse to be a replacement for your wife. I know you still love her, and I think that's admirable."

He felt his head nodding and wondered where this would go.

"Here are my demands. If I'm to be thrown into a marriage by my father's wishes, you will have to court me until we get married. It's the only wedding I intend to have, and I'm not going to walk into this one on Sunday, get up on Monday and make your breakfast and clean your house without some kind of happy memory to cling to."

"Demands?" He shoved his chair away from the table. "I don't—"

"Alma, I told you to give it time, and you'll fall in love with each other."

"You told her that, Doc? How can you promise her that?"

"Papa, it may or may not happen, and that's the way life is. Mr. Gibbons needs a mother for his girls more than he needs a wife, so I'm willing to do that. Before that happens, though, I want to be treated special. Right now, I feel like Mr. Gibbons ordered me from a catalog. He knows nothing about me or I him. It's only fair that I get to know him before we get married. I'm not asking for a year, only four weeks."

Miss Pickens had a good point. Roy settled his back against the chair. "What do you have in mind?"

"I'll make a list and give it to you when you pick me up for our first outing. You can choose where to take me." She rose from her chair and nodded. "This time tomorrow would be fine, unless you care to provide dinner?"

Roy's lips moved, though his mind couldn't grasp what he was saying. "Dinner. Yes, we have to eat."

"Tomorrow, then. Let me walk you to the door. I know you're needed at home, and I must work on my list."

Before he knew what had happened, Roy found himself escorted out by the pretty and spirited woman and left standing on the porch. How had she done that? Small as she was, he'd been moved to the door and hadn't felt a thing.

CHAPTER SIX

Alma checked the mirror again for stray hairs that may be out of place. She wouldn't admit it to anyone, but she was excited to be seeing Mr. Gibbons. Her cheeks couldn't hide that, flushed as they were against her pale skin.

Should she be waiting for him when he arrived or make him wait a little bit? She missed her mother. Her papa did his best, but when it came to being a female, he was lost.

Making him wait didn't feel comfortable. She should have asked Jewel what to do. She picked up the list, folded it, and stuck it in her dress pocket.

Her dress. Was it all right? She didn't put on her fanciest one but picked the blue wool one. It kept her warm, and Papa said it made her eyes bright as a July sky.

In the parlor, she settled on a chair. Papa had started a fire. He'd come home early to see her off. Most likely to make sure she would go with Mr. Gibbons.

"You look nice, my dear." Papa walked across the room and stoked the fire. "Mr. Gibbons should be here soon."

"Are you sure about this marriage, Papa? It's not too late. We haven't told anyone."

"I am."

"I understand you don't want me to come with you to St. Louis, and you rented out my home, but I could stay with Jewel and her husband. Or perhaps one of the widows from church? It's only for a year."

"No. I considered those things, but it's not fair to you. Suppose I find a wife in St. Louis. Then what will you do? You need your own home and family. A place where you can paint the furniture if you want to."

"I don't have to change things," Alma whispered.

"I want the best for you." He dabbed his eye and turned back to the fire.

Footsteps landed heavy on the wooden porch. There was a pause, then a knock. He was here. Why did her heart flip like a griddle cake? Goodness, she would need to get this emotion controlled before she faced him.

"That's your intended. I'll get the door, you wait here. A bit of mystery is a good thing. Your mother told me that. Guess I should have mentioned a few of those bits of wisdom to you sooner."

"There's still time, Papa."

"I love you, Little Bit. Don't forget that ever." He gave her a quick hug and released her.

"I won't. You're making me cry. My face will be all red."

"You're beautiful, like your mother." He stepped out of the room.

Alma blinked and looked at the ceiling to keep the tears from falling. She turned to see Mr. Gibbons standing in front of her father. He smiled. She caught the schoolgirl sigh before it escaped.

Roy had cleaned the carriage the best he could in the cold weather. He didn't think Miss Pickens would notice, but she sure would if it were a mess. "I hope you don't mind. We'll be dining at my house tonight. The girls are excited that you'll be eating with us." More than that, they'd been collecting pinecones after school and arranging them multiple ways across the tabletop.

"We're eating at your house?" Alma pivoted to look at him.

"That's what I said. The girls helped me set the table, even made some decorations, though I told them it's not a holiday."

"Nothing wrong with expressing creativity. It will be fun to see what they've come up with. Did they collect things from inside or outside?"

"You'll have to wait and see. They like you—the girls."

"I like them, too." She rubbed her hands together.

"Are you cold? I have a blanket if you need it." He reached behind her, tugged it over the carriage seat, and handed it to her.

Alma covered her lap and stuck her hands underneath. "Thank you. I should have brought my muff, but I didn't want to give in to it being winter yet. I dread its full-blown arrival."

"There, I've learned something about you. Winter is not your favorite season."

"I didn't say that. I love snow and ice skating, but the season lasts too long."

"I can never decide. In the heat of summer, I long for the cold. When it comes, I get tired of splitting wood and I want it to be July." He pulled up in front of the house, stopped the horse, and helped her out of the carriage.

Pete stepped out the door. "I'll take care of Dolly and get her in the barn. Those girls are wound tighter than a top. It'll be a rest to brush down the horse."

Inside, the girls wrapped their arms around Alma's waist.

"You came!" Frances said.

"Of course she did. Papa said she would," Elisbet said. "May I take your cloak, Miss Pickens?"

"Yes, you may. Thank you." Alma slid it from her shoulders and folded it in half before handing it to Elisbet. "There, maybe it won't be quite so hard to carry now."

His girls made him proud. "Thank you, Elisbet."

Elisbet buried her nose in the fabric and came up smiling. "You smell good, like cookies."

"And she has the most beautiful dress." Frances stroked the fabric. "Blue is my favorite color."

"Thank you." Alma's face flushed cranberry red.

Frances snuggled her hand into Alma's and tugged her toward the kitchen. "Come see the table."

Alma looked back at Roy. Was she trying to arch her eyebrow? He couldn't help but grin at her. He figured she didn't know how much his daughters craved a woman's attention. "I'll be right behind you." A place he didn't mind being, because his daughter was right. Alma smelled good.

Dinner went well. Alma exclaimed over the girls' efforts to make the kitchen "festive," as she called it. He hadn't seen Elisbet's face hold so much joy in months.

"Thank you for tucking them in while I checked on the calf."

"It was fun. I haven't read that princess book in years."

"I can't say the same. It's the same book, or a variation, every night. Think you'll be able to stand that after we're married?" He stood in the parlor. Should he sit next to her on the sofa or in the chair across from her? They'd sat together in the carriage, but that didn't count. Still, it was intimate sitting with a woman without a chaperone. Maybe he'd poke the fire again. "You mentioned a list?"

"I brought it with me." She slid her hand into her dress pocket and pulled out a folded paper. She did that little thing with her eyebrow that was a slight imitation of her father's. On Alma it was downright cute. "You won't toss it in the fire?"

"Maybe after I read it."

"Then sit next to me and I'll read it to you. That will eliminate the chance of its being destroyed." She patted the sofa. "The fire is fine. It's rather warm in here."

Was she bossy? Or practical? Janie never told him what to do. They'd married young, and she thought he could do anything. It had scared him to have someone think he was that capable. He'd let her down in the end. Maybe it would be better to have a wife with her own opinions, used to doing for herself. It would be harder to disappoint her.

He sat next to her, but not close enough to touch. "Let's hear the demands."

Alma unfolded the paper and held it up. "Isn't it pretty?"

The paper was bordered with tiny birds and flowers. Were those real pieces of ribbons glued to it? Roy nodded.

"I like to paint. I'm learning more about it, and I've been saving for the Oil Painting Outfit Complete with twenty-five colors of paint so I can increase my skills."

Her eyes were wide open and not at all showing any fear that he might disapprove. Not that he would. She'd find out soon enough how little time there would be to paint. "It's good to have something you love to do."

"I do love it. That's why it's on my list."

"Painting?"

"Yes, I want to paint the furniture."

Janie had picked out the furniture he hadn't made for them. "What's wrong with—" Alma dropped her gaze to the floor. He hadn't meant to hurt her, but those were changes he couldn't allow. He'd discuss it with her later.

Surely she would understand when he explained what the pieces meant to him. "What else is on that list?"

"First, I want a real wedding at the church, and after it, I want to have cake and punch for our friends. I can make my own wedding dress. Elisbet and Frances should have new ones, too, and shoes, maybe hair ribbons to match."

Roy grasped the paper and slipped it from her hand. "Let me read this." She wanted him to bring her flowers. Where did the woman think he was going to find flowers in November in Illinois? Did she think he had special growing powers that could make them bloom in the middle of winter? It became clear to him there might be a reason she hadn't married. He continued reading. Spend time together every day and . . . "Exchange special gifts at Christmas?" What did that mean?

CHAPTER SEVEN

Settled on Jewel's sofa, Alma and her friend hunched over a fashion plate in *Godey's Lady's Book*, admiring a dress.

Alma caressed the page. "It's perfect."

"You'll be beautiful. The bottle-green satin will make your eyes look bluer, and with the touches of red on the cuffs and inside the stand-up collar, it's perfect for Christmas."

"I think the cuffs should be red velvet."

"What about the hat?" Jewel wore a cat-grin.

"I'm not wearing a bird, especially a brown one!" Alma put her hands together on top of her head and flapped her fingers as if they were wings. "That would make quite a stir."

"I'm sure the bird is stuffed."

"Doesn't matter. Feathers are fine, but a dead bird is not." Alma frowned. "I have to find a gift for Mr. Gibbons, too." Why had she thought it would be a wonderful idea to make him a special present?

"Shouldn't you call him Roy?"

"I suppose. It feels too soon." And it was. Since she'd agreed to this marriage, her old life had disappeared. Precious objects were packed and stored; furniture had been moved as well. Papa had wasted no time readying to leave. Her body ached with sadness. "Jewel, this is the first time I won't be spending Christmas with Papa."

Jewel slid her arm around Alma's shoulder. "It's going to be fine. You'll be Mrs. Roy Gibbons on Christmas, and you'll have two excited daughters to wake you."

"I don't know what to make him."

"What does he like? What's his favorite color? You could knit a cap."

"I don't know. I wanted to do this because Mama and Papa did, but they were married almost a year before Christmas came." She, of course, had to do this the hard way. Meet a man, agree to marry him, and make him a meaningful gift in four weeks.

Jewel's son, Caleb, woke with a scream. "Time for me to go back to being a mother and not a schoolgirl. Why don't you ask around at the store and see if you can discover anything. Mrs. Remik up at the Star Store knows about everyone."

Alma felt light as relief pushed out the sadness. "She does!" She grabbed the Godey's *Lady's Book* and held it to her chest. "I'd love to stay and play with Caleb, but I have to go on a spying adventure."

Roy rode up to the front porch and slid down from the saddle. He was worked up about what he'd heard in town. He and Miss Pickens were in need of a serious talk. He rubbed the back of his neck. He'd fallen asleep reading to the girls last night and slept there for a few hours before realizing he wasn't in his own bed.

Alma opened the door with red-rimmed eyes. She'd been crying. His shoulders tensed as he waited for a problem to show up that he'd be expected to solve.

"Evening, Mr. Gibbons. Papa isn't home, so I can't let you in." She sniffed.

"He's a few minutes behind me. Told me to tell you not to keep me standing outside."

Alma backed away and held the door open. "I always honor my father's requests."

So that's what the crying was about. She still didn't want to marry him. He wasn't sure he wanted to marry her, either, but he'd shaken hands with her father. "It's time you started calling me Roy, don't you think?"

"I suppose so. . .Roy." She closed the door. "I've got dinner about ready to serve for Papa. Would you like some?"

"I came to talk to you, then I need to get home. Pete's with the girls, but I'm feeling bad about having him watch them so I can see you every night." She looked as if she might burst into tears. "Alma, that didn't come out right. Would you be agreeable to a few nights a week instead of—"

"No, I wouldn't. We need to know each other better."

"Is that why you've been asking around town what color shirts I like best and what I buy at the store?"

"Mrs. Remik told you?" Her eyes were wide as a doe's.

"Yes, and when she couldn't understand why you were so interested, I told her we were getting married."

"So now everyone in town knows." Her shoulders sagged as she turned away.

"They'll know soon, anyway. I don't see a problem."

"Of course not. Why would you? This is an arrangement between Papa and you. I don't have a choice."

"Is that why you've been crying, Alma?" His heart softened, and he put his hand on her shoulder. He prayed his daughters would never be in this situation. He would do his best from now on to make her feel treasured. Starting with taking her flowers, as soon as he could figure out some way to get some.

"No. It's because. . .I can't get my kitten heads to be round." She rested her hand on his for a moment, then brushed it away. "I need to stir. . .something."

Roy scratched his forehead and followed her into the kitchen. He would never understand women, but he knew enough not to ask about the kittens. When it came to females, he'd learned a small problem generally covered a bigger one.

Alma shivered on the porch step. Elisbet and Frances had rushed past her. "It's early. Why are you here, Roy?"

"I saw your father in town. He said you wouldn't be opposed to watching the girls. I've taken on extra work at the mill and won't be able to meet them after school."

"Papa said to bring them?" How was she to continue packing the house, making her dress, and figuring out what to give Roy for a gift with two little girls running around?

"He thought it'd be a good idea for you all to get to know each other better. He'll watch them while we sit in the parlor after dinner. Doc wants to get to know them, too. Since he'll be their grandfather."

"If he wants to be one, he should stay here in Trenton." She wrapped her arms tightly around her waist. Had he said supper? She needed to cook for all of them every night?

"Then, sweetheart"—he reached out and stroked her cheek—"we might not be getting married." Roy flashed his dimples, and then winked.

Sweetheart? Her knees went weak. Her body felt the way it did when she'd been double dosed with Mrs. Winslow's Soothing Syrup—all warm and happy. Did that mean. . . ? Could it be that he did care for her?

Chapter Eight

Ten inches of snow covered the ground. On his one day off in over a week, Roy ought to be inside doing chores. Instead, once again, he stood on Alma's porch at an odd time of day. Under a heavy blanket, his girls waited in the sleigh. Music-box giggles floated through the air.

Alma squealed with delight at the sight behind him. "Sleigh ride!"

"Would you like to go with us?" Was she bouncing on her toes? "Can you get ready fast? I don't want to undress those two while we wait. It takes too long to put them back together."

"I'll hurry!"

She meant it, because when she appeared less than five minutes later, the twist of hair on the nape of her neck was off center and the yellow ribbon didn't match the skirt he saw hanging from underneath her cloak. The fashionable Miss Pickens had turned into a little girl. She bounded past him, twisting a scarf around her neck. "How long can we ride?"

"Until the first one whines." He helped Alma into the sleigh and slid in next to her. When his arm brushed against hers, sparks he hadn't felt in a long time ignited. He urged the horse forward.

Alma rubbed her muffed hand under her chin. "It's the most beautiful thing, isn't it? Snow? Wouldn't it be perfect if there were bells on the sleigh, Elisbet?"

"Papa! Can we get bells?"

"Bells!" Frances chimed in.

"Please, don't encourage them." Roy glanced at Alma. "What's wrong with your eyebrow?"

"When Papa wants to make a point, he arches his. I can't, not yet. I'm training it." She used her finger to arch it. "Bells are not extravagant, if they make you happy."

Roy pursed his lips, then rolled them under. This was not a moment to laugh. "Look, there's a hill and sledders. The snow must be well packed. Anyone want to give it a try?"

A chorus of "I dos" rang from behind him.

He helped everyone from the sleigh and untied the wooden sled he'd brought. "Who's first?"

"Me!" Elisbet said.

"Me!" Frances jumped in front of Elisbet, lost her balance, and toppled in the snow.

"Me!" Alma helped Frances get up. "Let's make snow angels before we go home. That way we won't be as cold and can sled longer."

Alma took him by surprise. He hadn't imagined she'd want to fly down a snowy hill. "I think this sled can hold two, so Franny and I'll go first. Unless, Elisbet, you want to ride with her. She is covered in snow."

Roy lost track of how many runs Alma and the girls, even he, made down the hill. Finally he had to say, "I think it's time to go."

"No, you have to ride with Miss Pickens!" Elisbet insisted.

He started to refuse, but Alma had already climbed on the sled. He settled behind her, the closeness of her, the sweet scent of her hair clutching his heart. Before he let his mind run off the rails, he sent the sled down the hill and into a snow bank. Snow covered her face. Before he could help her up, she giggled, then went into a full-throttle laugh, fell backward, and made a snow angel.

"I want to do that again!"

"Maybe next time. I think it's best to get all the red-checked women in my life home and warmed up so there aren't any more colds." He couldn't handle another close ride with her. Not until they were married, anyway.

He loaded everyone on the sleigh, then went to attach the sled to the back. On his way, he noticed a yellow ribbon. He picked it up and slid it into his pocket with a smile. He had his first piece of the gift he'd make Alma.

In the Gibbonses' warm kitchen, Alma yanked on Frances's boot until it gave up and released her foot. "Your stockings are wet. Are yours, Elisbet?"

Elisbet nodded.

"Let's find dry clothes for you two before you catch a chill. While we're gone, Roy, could you make some hot chocolate for us?"

"You have to say please." Frances's teeth chattered.

"Please." Alma bent down in front of Frances. "You're right. I should have said that." She stood and took the child's hand. "Shall we?"

Once Alma had the girls in warm clothes, they returned to the kitchen. She'd brought along their brush. "Frances, you're first. Let's get the knots out of your hair." The little girl stood still while her hair was put back in order.

Elisbet took her place. "You hurt less than Papa."

"I've had years of practice unsnarling hair."

"That's true. My hair has never been that long and won't be. Enjoy it, girls, because it's still a few weeks until Christmas."

"And we get Miss Pickens for our mama!" Frances shouted.

"Settle down. The cocoa is ready." He ladled it into cups.

The girls slid into their chairs. Chilled, Alma hesitated. She wanted to sit next to the stove, but that was Roy's seat.

"Sit here," Elisbet demanded, then added, "please."

Roy set cups in front of Frances and Elisbet. "Yes, that's a good spot for you. I'm sure you're cold and wet, too. We should have taken you home first."

"I don't mind. I only did one snow angel, so I wasn't as wet as these two."

Roy placed a cup in front of her. "This will help warm you. Good suggestion, Janie."

If a heart could make a sound when it broke, Alma's would have. Janie. His dead wife's name. She wanted to disappear, be anywhere but Roy Gibbons's kitchen. Her throat closed.

Roy's pale face swam through her watery eyes. "Alma, I'm so sorry. For a moment it felt like we were a family, and I guess that's why I called you Janie. You've filled a vacancy today, and my heart felt whole. Thank you. Can you forgive me, Alma?"

"Is Papa in trouble?" Frances hopped from her chair and was by his side, hot chocolate forgotten.

"No. Everything is fine." Alma offered a forced smile, but looked away from Roy. It wasn't good that he took her as a replacement for Janie. He had to understand that before they married. She wasn't sure he would. She loved his children, but Roy never spent time alone with her. He didn't want a wife, he wanted a caretaker. "I am feeling chilled. Would you take me home now?"

Roy could have kicked himself. He had called her Janie. Alma had done her best not to let him touch her while he helped her into her cloak. He had to make this better. He could have offered her dry clothes, but that wouldn't do.

She wouldn't want to wear the dress of Janie's that he'd kept.

Once in the sleigh, he thought he'd go for distraction. It worked for his daughters. Maybe it would for Alma. "Have you considered what you'd like to bring to the house?"

"My painting equipment, and Papa offered Mama's china. I'd like to bring it." She spoke to the side of the sleigh instead of turning his way.

"We'll probably find a place to store things in the barn. Janie's china is still serviceable, and I'm not sure where we'd put your paints."

"As you wish."

This wasn't going well. He'd planned to kiss her when he took her home, but now? He'd best wait.

CHAPTER NINE

Something roused Roy. Had Frances cried out? He pushed against the chair arms and rose. He didn't hear her now.

He was heartsick about calling Alma the wrong name. Even thought of getting Pete to watch the girls so he could go talk to her. Get her to understand he liked having her in his kitchen. Instead, after getting the girls down for the night, he had sat down to rest and had drifted off.

A knock sounded. "Gibbons!"

Roy jerked open the door. "Dr. Pickens. Is Alma all right?"

"No, she is not." Dr. Pickens marched past him. "I thought you were a decent man." He paced the room. "I'm giving you my most valuable possession because I thought you were worthy. It seems I'm wrong."

"Doc, can I—"

"No sir, you cannot. I have a lot to say. My little girl has been in her room since you brought her home. She's crying, and I can't make her stop." He faced Roy. "Do you know how that feels?"

Not sure if he was allowed to speak, Roy just nodded.

"I know you do, because you've been raising those girls alone. That's why this match is a good one. You need each other, but you can't be calling my Alma by your wife's name." He lowered himself into a chair. "Now, what is your explanation?"

Roy sat across from the doctor, dipped his head, and held his forehead with his hands. "It slipped out. Everything felt normal, like we were a family again. I tried to tell her that."

"She doesn't expect you to quit loving Janie. She knows what it's like to lose someone you love, but son, you have to do what your vows said."

What vows? He and Alma hadn't said any yet. Confused, Roy straightened his back and gaped at him.

"Remember the part that says, 'until death do us part'? You have to release Janie and let Alma move into your heart. She needs the bigger space now. Show her you care enough to remember her name. All this coming over to our house in the evening is nice, but it's not enough. Alma was right. You need to court her so you mean it when you say those vows to her. You better repair this mess right away. Otherwise, you might as well hire a woman to come help in this house."

"I took her sledding."

"With your children."

"She didn't mind." He stopped from squirming like a ten-year-old caught with his hand in the cookie jar. Why had he thought this would be easy? Alma didn't know him, and he shouldn't expect her to.

"Take her out alone. There's always a bonfire on the weekend down by the pond at Sauer's place. Bring her candy. Take her ice skating. Hold her hand. Stare into her eyes. Make her feel like she's the only one in the world. Janie agreed to marry you, so you must know how to court a woman. Do you remember?"

Yes, he did, and the memory hurt. Could he do those things with Alma?

Alma's heart wasn't in making Roy's gift. She'd failed to find out more about him. She knew he cared about his family, but beyond that, she hadn't even discovered his favorite color. She strolled the store aisle searching for something to use to craft an ornament.

She fingered silk ribbons. Elisbet and Frances would like these. They were easy to buy for, not like their father. If God would send her an idea of what to make, something Roy would save and treasure, she'd be grateful.

The door opened, and the sunlight struck something, sending a rainbow through the room. She picked up her pace. And there it was. A beautiful, clear, glass teardrop ornament. The perfect size for painting. She purchased it along with the ribbons and hurried home as the sun set.

She slowed her step. Roy sat on the porch rail waiting for her.

"I heard there was a bonfire tonight. I'd like to take you, just you, if you'll go with me," he asked.

Thrilled, Alma ran upstairs and put away her purchases, found warm clothes, and met him at the door. Minutes later they were at Sauer's pond, sitting by a bonfire and lacing on their skates. He'd said little to her on the ride and even now remained quiet. Maybe it was time for her to let go of her anger and give him an opportunity to start over.

She could either continue to be furious or take it as a compliment that Roy was comfortable with her. The fire crackled and popped behind her. "Are we going to be like the wild young ones and take a chance on the ice, or stay by the fire like our elders?"

Roy's eyes flashed in the firelight. Then he took her hand. "I'm not feeling like an elder, so let's be young, but not wild. Unless you want to be?"

Was that uncertainty or fear in his voice? "Not up to falling and spinning on the ice tonight?"

"Not when I have to be a father in the morning. If I could lie around in bed like you all day, counting the flowers on the wallpaper, then I might."

She playfully slapped his arm. "I have never lain in bed all day."

"What do you do with your days?"

"Lots of things. Paint, feed the chickens, gather feathers for projects." Alma waved at her friend Katie and her brother as they swished by. "Make dinner for Papa."

"Feathers? What do you do with them?"

"I'm working on a dye to color them, or sometimes I try to paint them." Her foot slipped. "Oh!"

Roy caught her, brought her upright, and steadied her. "You paint them and then what?"

"I haven't found the best application for them, yet. They may have something to do with your special Christmas gift." She gave her best mystery-smile and skated away. Feathers. Perhaps she could find some way to adhere them to his gift.

Roy circled her, then slipped in next to her, taking her hand. "Want to play a game?"

She attempted the eyebrow arch and felt it go a tiny bit higher. "What kind?"

"A getting-to-know-you game. I'll give you two choices and you guess which one I like. Then you get a turn."

"I'm first." She dropped his hand, skated ahead and did a spin, and returned with a question. "Christmas or Fourth of July?"

"You like Christmas because we'll be married by then."

"I do like it best, but not because we'll be married. I love the Nativity story and that's when Jesus was born."

"I like that you'll be my wife and you get to be there when the girls jump out of bed and their eyes are wide with excitement. I can't wait for you to see that."

The thin layer of ice around her heart began to drip. He did want to marry her. He'd said that first before anything else. She should apologize for leaving in a huff the other day. Roy pulled her tightly to him as they rounded the end of the frozen pond. "Working in the field or with wood?"

"I think"—she tilted her head and studied his face—"the field, because it provides for your family."

"Both do, and while I'm grateful, the fields don't provide much enjoyment. I like making things out of wood."

"So my gift is made of wood?" She giggled.

"Still a secret. You might be getting nothing more than a splinter."

"Orange or black?"

"Odd choices for favorite colors. Orange?"

"Black. I like black cats." A small group of boys began to race on the ice, whizzing past at dizzying speeds. The bonfire looked appealing.

"Cats make me sneeze. Do you think I'd rather eat pork chops or roast and potatoes?"

"Pork chops."

"Roast, because the next day I can have a delicious sandwich. I haven't had a good roast not since Janie—"

A few boys raced past. One tripped, and his arms went in wild circles as he attempted to stay on his feet. He fell, sliding in their direction. Alma squealed.

Roy whipped Alma away from the sharp blades before they reached her. She ought to be grateful, but all she remembered was hearing the name Janie—again.

In the barn, Roy caressed a piece of wood. He had to prove to Alma he cared. He'd seen the look on her face when he'd mentioned Janie again. If he wanted, and he did, to build a life with her, he needed to start with a good foundation.

He hadn't lied to her when he'd said she'd get a splinter for Christmas, because she surely would. But it wasn't her only gift. He had the special one finished, ready for Christmas.

Chapter Ten

"Remember, you can't tell your father about this."
Alma tied Frances's apron and then checked to make sure
Elisbet was well covered.

Before the girls arrived, Alma had covered the kitchen
table with last week's *Trenton Gazette* to protect it from
the red and green paint she'd mixed for them to use.

"We won't." Elisbet shoved her fists under her chin and
squealed. "We keep secrets, don't we, Franny?"

"Yeth." Franny gave a missing-tooth grin. Her front
tooth had fallen out last week, making her even more
adorable.

Alma was unsure about these two. They tended to tell
their father about their day the moment they saw him.
"Let's sit at the kitchen table. Be careful—" They were in
their chairs, feet kicking against the bottom rungs before
she finished her sentence. "Not to knock over the paint."

"What are we painting?" Elisbet turned in her chair. "I
don't see anything worth keeping a secret."

"I get the green!" Frances shouted.

"Frances, no yelling. There is enough of both colors. Turn back around, Elisbet. What we are painting is in my apron pocket."

The room grew quiet as Alma reached into her pocket and withdrew the ornament wrapped in brown paper. "This is it." She sat between them, set the package on the table, and lifted an edge of the paper, gently unwinding it. "It's made of glass. We have to be careful."

Alma held the ornament up for them to see. "We are going to paint our names on it. What do you think?"

No response. No excitement. No anything. She looked at each girl. No smiles. "What's wrong?"

"Franny can't write her name."

"I'll help her. Would that be okay, Frances?"

"Yeth. Can we paint the paper, too?"

"That's a good idea. While Elisbet paints her name on the ornament, you can work on half of the wrapping paper. Then we can switch."

The girls worked with occasional giggles, and Alma had to wipe paint from the ends of their hair a few times.

"Finished!" Frances glowed. "All my letterth are on there."

Including an adorable fingerprint. Alma didn't know if Roy would cherish it, but she would.

"Can we put your name and Papa's on it?" Elisbet asked. "Because Papa said we're going to be a family. So, can we?"

Alma's heart swelled with love. "Yes, and we'll hang it on our tree every year."

She finished the last stroke on Roy's *y*. The back door swung open. Her father rushed in, breathless. "The church is on fire. The wedding's canceled. Roy's on his way. Meet him at the front door, and I'll hide this."

"We are getting married." Roy shivered in the cold air. The water on his pants had turned to ice. "Can I come in?"

"Yes, of course. You're wet. Go in the parlor where it's warm. I'll get hot chocolate for you, to chase the chill."

"I want—need you to come with me." He grasped her hand and pulled her along with him. Standing with his back to the fire, willing his teeth not to chatter, he drew her close and kissed her. "Alma Gail Pickens, will you marry me?"

"I don't under—"

"Just answer the question."

"Yes."

Her face crinkled and her eyebrow arched. Did she realize it? He wanted to laugh and then shout, "I love Alma Pickens!"

"Roy?" Her questioning eyes begged for more.

He kissed her again, feeling the heat thaw his lips. "I saw the church in flames, and I knew the wedding would be called off. Then I realized, if this had happened tomorrow while we were there, I might have lost you, and I haven't told you how I feel. That I love the way you make every activity fun, the way you practice your eyebrow arch, and the way you make me feel like more than a father. You've given me my life back, and I never even proposed to you. You deserve that. So I'll ask you again, Alma, would you marry me? Could you love me for the rest of our lives?"

"Yes! I love you, too. But how will we get married? The girls are counting on having a mother on Christmas morning."

"Don't worry. I have a plan. If you keep Elisbet and Frances tonight, I promise to make tomorrow a special memory, even without the church." He tipped her head and kissed her again.

"Are you going to kiss me a lot when we're married?"

"Yes, I am."

"I'm glad. I didn't know I'd like it so much." Her face flushed a bright red. "I should get you something to drink, to warm you."

"I don't need anything. You've thawed my frozen bones, sweetheart."

Alma waited in Roy's bedroom, trying hard not to think that it would be her bedroom, too, tonight. Her father had covered her eyes when they entered the house, and the girls led her in so she couldn't see the decorations. Her hands shook. How she wished Mama were here. Jewel had explained a few things to her, with a scarlet face. Her father had come to her room last night to discuss with her the duties of a wife. Horrified, she'd sent him away.

She'd helped Elisbet and Frances into their red velvet dresses and tied bows in their hair. Their faces were blinding with joy as they scooted from the room. Jewel had helped her put on her dress. The satin, soft as a kitten, slid over her head. She rubbed the red velvet cuff between her fingers. It was perfect. Even more so, she knew she would honor her mother and father by marrying Roy.

It was almost time. Soon she'd be Mrs. Roy Gibbons. Her stomach twirled. She promised God she would be the best wife and mother possible. The door opened, and her father stepped inside, beaming.

He held out his arm. "You're beautiful, Little Bit. So much like your mother. Are you ready?"

Alma took his elbow, and they strolled past the dining room. Roy had placed Mama's embroidered tablecloth under heaping platters of bread and meat. China dishes and. . .were those Mama's cups? They were. Her eyes watered. It felt right, almost as if Mama were here, smiling. It was beautiful, festive.

But the parlor took her breath away. Candles in crystal holders ambled across the mantel, sending warm, dancing lights across the room. A music box played in the background, and Roy waited for her by the fire with the preacher. He'd kept his promise. He'd given her a wedding to remember.

The bedroom door creaked. Alma started. She heard giggles and opened her eyes.

"Good morning, Mrs. Gibbons." Roy stood inside the door, holding tight to his daughters' shoulders. "They have something to say." He let go, and blond hair flew as Elisbet and Frances ran and jumped on the bed.

Elisbet tapped Frances's shoulder. "One, two, three."

"Merry Christmas, Mama!" Alma treasured the unison of the sweet voices.

"Come on, girls, let's let your mama get dressed and meet us in the parlor."

Alma smiled at her new husband with gratitude.

The girls waited by the tree, pointing out decorations they liked. They asked questions about how the tree got into the house without them knowing, and when could they open presents. They were elated at the ribbons from Alma and the gifts from Roy.

"Mrs. Gibbons? I believe you are to give me a special gift?"

Alma giggled. "It's here." She hopped to her feet and brought out a package.

"We painted the paper!" Frances shouted. "And we—"

"Hush, Franny." Elisbet covered Frances's mouth. "You're giving it away. Open it, Papa!"

"Remove your hand from your sister's mouth, please." Roy unwrapped the ornament and, if possible, the dimples in his cheeks grew deeper as he smiled.

"Do you like it?" Alma thought so, but wanted to hear him say it.

"I do. I see our names and one fingerprint. The feather is a nice touch. That's from you, Alma?"

"Yes, and the fingerprint is from Frances. I thought it was special."

"It is, and we will cherish this. One day, this will hang on your tree, Frances."

Elisbet frowned. "Why does she get to have it?"

"Just wait." Roy drew a package from his pocket. "Here is my gift, Alma."

She opened the paper. Inside was an ornament made of blond braided hair shaped into a heart and glued to a small piece of wood. A yellow ribbon twisted with a piece of a black string tie wove through a hole and tied to use as a hanger. "Is this my ribbon?"

"And my tie. I wanted this gift to represent our family."

"I love it." Alma pressed it to her heart. "Elisbet, someday this will be yours."

Later, Roy slipped a kiss on Alma's neck. "Remember when I said you were going to get a splinter for Christmas?"

"But I didn't. You sanded the wood smoothly."

"I made you something else." Roy's heart beat fast, ready to explode.

Alma's face filled with excitement.

"Come to the barn with me." Once they were inside, he led her to a stall and yanked off the tattered quilt covering the blanket chest he'd built. "I wanted to start this marriage off with a piece of furniture we both made. I've done my part. Now it's up to you to paint it any way you like."

Alma dropped to her knees. She ran her hand across the daises he'd carved on the front panel. "Daisies."

"To get you through the winter until I can bring you real ones."

"It's so beautiful." She opened the lid and gasped. "The Oil Painting Outfit Complete!" She jumped up and wrapped her arms around him. "I love you, Roy Gibbons."

"I love you, too." She fit him more perfectly than he ever could have imagined. God had replaced his pain and loss with Alma, who taught him true love could come more than once in a lifetime.

<div align="center">~~~</div>

Dear Reader,

Thank you for taking this journey with Alma and Roy. What's next for the town of Trenton? Emmie Mueller is hatching up matchmaking plans in Matchmaker Bride. She doesn't expect her plan to be used on her! The Matchmaker Bride preview is below.

If you would please sign up for Diana's newsletter so you won't miss the arrival of new books. Tap here to sign up! http://dianabrandmeyer.com/back-of-outlaw-subscribe/

She's the best matchmaker in town... Or is she?

CHAPTER ELEVEN

EMMIE MUELLER WORE HER favorite floral dress to the July wedding. She hoped the skirt wouldn't wilt in the humidity. Two old bachelors down and two to go, and then she and Granny would be on their way to Kansas to be with their family.

Orville Tinze, the first bachelor she made a match for, had bluebonnet eyes and soft manners, which made him attractive to several older widows. In less than a month, he said his vows.

Getting today's happy couple together had been the most difficult task. A nigh impossible endeavor. But with God's help, she'd found a wife for George Henderson. One Sunday, she noticed the church organist, spinster Louise Wheeler, sending longing looks toward George. The surly old man would never have picked up on those subtle glances. But Emmie did, and she took action.

With a little coaxing, she managed to get George looking quite dapper before she put the two of them together at the church voters' meeting. He took to Louise like rain on a parched garden.

Finding the other two boarders a spouse couldn't be as tiresome. Her cheeks hurt from smiling.

"Do you take. . ."

She brought her attention back to the vows. This had to be the best part of the wedding, when two people in love promised to be together forever. And to think, God used her to bring this about. This must be God approving her plan to find matches for the other gentlemen boarders.

Hylda Mueller, Emmie's grandmother, nudged her in the side and leaned close to her ear. "Someday that will be you."

A rush of heat rose to her face. "Shh, Granny." Sometimes her grandmother spoke too loud, and when Mrs. Thompson snickered behind them, Emmie feared this was one of those times.

Granny patted her leg and nodded.

The couple faced the congregation, and the pastor introduced the newlyweds. Both of them beamed through their wrinkles. Satisfied everyone had their attention on the couple, Emmie slipped out the side of the pew. The finishing touches for the reception being held in the side yard of the church needed to be readied.

Landon Knipp left the building he was considering renting in Lebanon, Illinois, thankful his father had come along with him to inspect it. This one, unlike others they'd explored, appeared to be the right size for his specialty market and in the right location on the corner of Main and Spruce.

Mr. Knipp brushed dust particles from his jacket sleeve. "You don't need to move. Why not stay in St. Louis and work with the family? It's a headache to start a new place where you aren't known."

"Father, whether you believe it or not, as the youngest, I'll never have a chance to be the boss. I've spent my entire life being ordered around by my brothers. I'd like to try being the one in charge." Landon stepped back to inspect the front overhang. "No light peeking through."

"Where do you plan to live?"

"Maybe above the store. That would give me a bit more money to put into this place, maybe on better display cases." Landon shaded his eyes and peered down the busy street crowded with farm wagons and buggies. Another good indication that his store would have customers.

Church bells jangled in an unordered tune, as if a few schoolboys had control of the rope.

"Is it the top of the hour already?" His father checked his pocket watch. "No, not even close. There must be something happening at the church."

"Sounds like it's around the corner. Let's walk in that direction. This building is only one part of my life. I'll need to find a church. Worshipping is important as well."

And finding a wife.

All six of his married brothers had at least one child. When he'd returned from Europe, he'd been surrounded by infants and toddlers. Each one brought a distinct desire in him to have a family of his own. And to stay in one town. No more traveling for him.

If the bells didn't lead them to church, the steeple would have. The redbrick building was simple in appearance except for the stained-glass circular window above the double entry doors. Though it wasn't as grand as those in Europe or back East. Even St. Louis had more impressive houses of worship.

The side yard contained tables decorated with many different cloths and flowers. "I'd say it's a wedding." Landon stopped at the bottom of the steps.

The door flew open. A blond-haired beauty hurried through it and down the steps.

"Do you suppose that's the bride?" His father snickered.

Emmie's narrow-skirted dress hindered her movement. Now she regretted wearing it, instead of the wide skirt she wore at home. Going slow down the stairs wasted time she needed to uncover the food.

On the last step, she stumbled.

Her ankle twinged.

She grasped for something to steady her, but found air.

Someone grabbed her by the waist, and she fell into the arms of a man. One she'd never met. Emmie swallowed. Was her embarrassment from the fall? Before she could sort out her feelings, he righted her and then tipped his hat.

"Landon Knipp."

"Thank you for saving me, Mr. Knipp. I'm afraid my mind was on getting the tables ready for the wedding guests." She smoothed the skirt at her waist.

"Then you aren't the bride?"

She hadn't noticed the older man standing next to Mr. Knipp.

"Father. Excuse him, Miss. . . ?"

"Miss Mueller." She turned to the older gentleman. "No, sir, I'm a helper today."

"My father has an odd sense of humor."

"I see. Well, if you don't mind, I need to get busy." She took a step and winced. "Ow."

He grasped her by the arm. "Here, lean on me, and I'll get you to the tables. You can sit and rest and direct Father and me on what needs to be done."

"I couldn't, shouldn't. . ."

"She's right, son. We aren't guests at this wedding."

"We won't stay. With the two of us, we'll get things shipshape in no time. Miss Mueller?"

If they hurried, there might be a chance. And she did want George and Alice to have a beautiful day. "Please, that would be kind of you, and then you can be on your way." They would have to finish before Granny saw him, or there'd be wedding suggestions before they made it home. Having a new man in town would ignite the fire under Granny, and the pressure to marry would be upon her once again.

CHAPTER TWELVE

LANDON UNCOVERED THE THIRD dish of potato salad and moved it down to a table next to the other two bowls. That was the last one. He stepped back to inspect the display. Finished and grouped like with like. He and his father did a decent job of making the tables appealing. A feast for the stomach and the eyes. Would Miss Mueller think so? He glanced at her. She rubbed her ankle. It would be blue and purple by evening.

A loud cheer rose from the front of the church. The newlyweds and their guests would be coming this way soon. He headed over to Miss Mueller. "We're finished. Is there anything else you'd like us to do?"

"You've done a marvelous job. I wouldn't have considered placing the foods the way you have. We usually let the person bringing something set it where they want it."

"It makes more sense to have all the potato salad in one place, doesn't it?" He scratched his chin.

She wrinkled her forehead and chewed her lip.

"Unless there is a reason?"

"There is. It's a tradition passed down from generations. If one has all the bowls together, someone might get their feelings hurt if their bowl isn't touched. And sometimes people forget to put something on their plate, and they have a second chance of doing so as they move down the row."

"We should move them around then. I'll get Father—"

Her eyes widened, and she looked past him.

"Emmie, who is this?"

He turned to find an older woman standing behind him. "I'm Landon Knipp, ma'am. My father and I helped Miss Mueller set out the food."

"They aren't staying, Granny. They offered to help when I misstepped and twisted my ankle." She stood, wobbled, and caught the edge of the table to steady herself.

"Nonsense. You helped my granddaughter, and you must stay. There's plenty of food." The older woman beamed. "We love having new people attend our church. Where are you from?"

"St. Louis." His father stepped next to him. "My son is looking at a building to open his new business."

"What do you do, Mr. Knipp?"

"If I decide to settle here, my store will carry items you can't find at the mercantile. My father owns Knipp Emporium in St. Louis. And I'm opening our second one."

"What does that mean? Things I can't find at the mercantile?" Emmie narrowed her eyes.

Landon's heart stuttered. He'd insulted her town and her. "Items from all over the world. Fine china, exotic spices from India, that sort of thing. When a customer walks in, we want them to be wide-eyed and speechless while they take in the displays."

"Followed by excitement. Don't forget that, Landon. Lest the ladies think you want them to be as quiet as a church mouse while they shop." His father chuckled.

"You won't be competing against the mercantile, then?"

"Not at all. Our intent is to have different choices. Not everyone gets to travel around the world purchasing items to decorate their homes or give as gifts. Like this." Landon pulled a handkerchief stitched with embroidered birds from his pocket and handed it to her.

She traced the stitching. "It's beautiful. You're right. I haven't seen anything like this before."

"Our store will be filled with items like this."

"Look, Granny, isn't this exotic?"

Mrs. Mueller held it in her hands and rubbed the fabric between her thumb and finger. "The fabric is soft as down."

"You will do well with a store in this town. When will you decide?" Mrs. Mueller cocked her head. "And where do you plan on living?"

Emmie knew what was coming before Granny asked. She wanted a boarder to fill George's room. "Granny! That's none of our business."

"It certainly is. Did you forget we run a boarding-house?"

She squirmed like a little girl under Granny's glare. "No, but remember—"

"This is not the time or place to discuss this." She turned to them. "If you are in need of a place to stay, please come see us. We have plenty of rooms available."

Rooms she'd worked hard at emptying of boarders. She knew Granny didn't want to leave this town, but it wasn't fair of her to expect Emmie to stay here. She wanted to be with her family, and that included Granny. Yes, she did want to marry and have children, but not here. No, she did not. She wanted to be near her momma. But Momma wouldn't approve of her pouting. She gathered her emotions and tucked them away.

"Mr. Landon, it would be an honor if you'd stay with us for a short time." *Please turn down the offer.*

"Thank you, but Father and I will return to St. Louis this afternoon. I have some decisions to make. I've seen several towns that fit my needs."

His words were like warm butter, and the tension in her shoulders dissolved. A problem diverted, though looking at him again, it wouldn't be hard to find him a wife if he did stay. Handsome, with those Jersey-cow eyes framed with long, dark lashes. Yes, there would be a few women in town that would want to sit at his table every night. Good thing he was leaving, because she might be tempted to get his attention and that would mess up her plan.

There were quite a few people at the reception. Landon listened in on conversations as he filled his plate, hoping to get a feel for the people of the town.

"Something's going on, Walter. I think Emmie is up to some shenanigans."

Hearing Emmie's name, he whipped around and took note of the two older men behind him in line.

"Milton, I'm telling you. Orville getting married didn't surprise me. He still has all his hair. But George? Didn't you notice how Miss Emmie got him to slick down his hair and make sure his mustache didn't have food in it every Sunday?"

"You might be right. Do you think she's trying to match us up, too?"

"We best keep an eye on her. I like things the way they are." Milton plopped potato salad onto his plate.

"Landon?" His father spoke into his ear. "You are listening in on conversations again?"

"Yes. You can learn a lot about the culture of a place when you do that."

"You're in Illinois, son, not a foreign land. Not much different from where you grew up. Let's look for a place to sit."

Under a young tree, they found a spot that hadn't been claimed and settled beneath it with their packed plates. From here, Landon observed Miss Emmie Mueller undetected. Her delicate fingers piano-key danced through the air while she chatted with another woman.

"She's a pretty one with that blond hair." His father wiggled his fork in her direction. "Are you thinking this town might offer you more than a place to sell wares from abroad?"

"You know me too well. But it's not just her. I know nothing about her. It's the townspeople that will be the key to having a successful business. Like those celebrating this wedding. I should think them to be an indication of the type of people I'd be selling to."

Miss Mueller filled her own plate even with an injured ankle. He noticed. Yes, he did. He'd been watching for a beau to offer her assistance, but none came. Maybe she didn't have one. Curious that one so beautiful wouldn't have a group of bachelors hanging around trying to capture a smile from her.

"—and you'd need furniture, too." His father's words broke into his thoughts.

"Pardon? My mind drifted somewhere."

"I thought as much. I've been observing your keen interest in the young Miss Mueller. Your fork has been hovering over that piece of ham for quite some time." His father raised his eyebrow. "What interests you the most about her?"

He stabbed the piece of meat and stuck it in his mouth, debating whether to answer his father's question.

"You're stalling, son." He laughed loud enough for a group to turn and stare.

Landon tipped his hat at them. "She must be a member of this church, as she is talking to everyone. One of my high priorities. I desire a marriage such as my brothers' and yours. This might be the best town we've seen to open the store." And Emmie Mueller, the possible matchmaker, was the first woman he wanted to get to know.

Get *Matchmaker Bride* here https://books2read.com/matchmakerbride

Chapter Thirteen

Diana Lesire Brandmeyer writes historical and contemporary romances. She is the CBA best-selling author of *Mind of Her Own*, *A Bride's Dilemma in Friendship, Tennessee*, and *We're Not Blended*. Once widowed and now remarried, she writes with humor and experience on the difficulty of joining two families, be it fictional or real life.

Please visit her webpage, www.dianabrandmeyer.com and sign up for her newsletter

Contemporary
Silverton Lake Romances

A Time to Dance Silverton A Lake Romance Book 1

A Time to Bake A Silverton Lake Romance Book 2

A Time to Heal A Silverton Lake Romance Book 3
Stand-Alones

Mind of Her Own

Hearts on the Road
Historical
Small Town Brides

Love Finds an Outlaw

The Christmas Wish

Matchmaker Bride

The Honey Bride

From a Distance
Frontier Legacy Brides

A Bride's Dilemma in Friendship, Tennessee

A Bride's Journey to the Colorado Territory

A Bride's Choice in Central City

www.ingramcontent.com/pod-product-compliance
Lightning Source LLC
Chambersburg PA
CBHW060443160726

47992CB00003B/1052